D0041623

WITHDRAWN

Attack of the Giant Octopus

Don't miss the other spine-tingling
Secrets of Dripping Fang adventures!

BOOK ONE:
The Onts

BOOK TWO:
Treachery and Betrayal at Jolly Days

BOOK THREE:
The Vampire's Curse

BOOK FOUR:
Fall of the House of Mandible

BOOK FIVE:
The Shluffmuffin Boy Is History

SECRETS OF

DRIPPING FANG

BOOK SIX

Attack of the Giant Octopus

DAN GREENBURG

Illustrations by SCOTT M. FISCHER

HARCOURT, INC.

Orlando Austin New [illegible] Toronto London

I want to thank my editor, Allyn Johnston, for her macabre yet soulful sense of humor, for her eagerness to explore ideas beyond the bounds of taste, for understanding an author's poignant thirst for praise, and for helping me say exactly what I'm trying to say, except more gooder.
I also want to thank Scott M. Fischer,
an artist with dizzying technical abilities and a demented genius at combining terror and humor in the same illustration.
—D. G.

www.HarcourtBooks.com

Library of Congress Cataloging-in-Publication Data
Greenburg, Dan.
Secrets of Dripping Fang. Book six, Attack of the giant octopus/
Dan Greenburg; illustrations by Scott M. Fischer.—1st ed.
p. cm.
Summary: When the babies who are being fed on human snot mutate into half-human brats, Hedy Mandible uses her hypnotic control over Cheyenne to force her to teach them proper behavior, while the Jackal initiates another elaborate scheme to assassinate Wally.
[1. Orphans—Fiction. 2. Twins—Fiction. 3. Brothers and sisters—Fiction. 4. Swamps—Fiction. 5. Ants—Fiction. 6. Vampires—Fiction. 7. Cincinnati (Ohio)—Fiction.] I. Fischer, Scott M., ill. II. Title. III. Title: Attack of the giant octopus.
PZ7.G8278Seg 2007
[Fic]—dc22 2006015517
ISBN-13: 978-0-15-206041-1 ISBN-10: 0-15-206041-3

Text set in Meridien
Designed by Linda Lockowitz

First edition
A C E G H F D B

Printed in the United States of America

For Judith and Zack

with spooky love

—D. G.

Contents

CHAPTER 1

I'd Like an Appointment with the Giant Octopus, Please

Midnight in the basement of Cincinnati's Horace Hotchkiss Aquarium. Puddles on the concrete floor. The festering smell of a fish market on a hot day.

"Keep your trap shut and follow me," warned a voice in a harsh whisper.

The Jackal, a figure in a black leather trench coat, turned toward the voice. It had come from a man wearing a wet rubber scuba suit dripping with slime.

It was the job of the man in the scuba suit dripping with slime to clean the giant tanks in which the aquarium's most dangerous inhabitants were imprisoned. The man's name was Sledge. He had a two-day growth of beard and a deeply scarred face, the result of confrontations with creatures that didn't appreciate his housecleaning. A large part of Sledge's lower right lip was missing, revealing a disturbing sneer of teeth. It was fortunate he worked nights and rarely came in contact with the public.

Sledge led The Jackal into a dimly lit storage room. On its floor, black hoses coiled like sea snakes.

"Okay, chief, tell me what you want," said Sledge, his voice as low and deep as a foghorn. "But make it snappy—I don't have all night."

Deliberately taking more time than he needed to, The Jackal removed a stiff pack of stinky French cigarettes from his trench coat pocket, put one between his lips, set it on fire with a wooden match, inhaled deeply, then exhaled a cloud of putrid smoke.

"One evening after the aquarium has closed," said The Jackal, "a friend of mine, a young man, a professional daredevil, wishes to enter the tank with your giant octopus."

"Absolutely, positively, totally, and completely out of the question," the tank cleaner snapped.

"What a pity," said The Jackal, puffing on his cigarette. "Why?"

"Why?" Sledge snorted, laughing nastily. "The octopus would snake her tentacles around your friend's body and squeeze him like a tube of toothpaste. Her beak would open him up like a can of sardines, and she'd feast on his guts. His screams would die inside big bubbles of air. A truly ghastly death."

"My friend is, of course, aware of the risk," said The Jackal, inhaling more smoke from his vile French cigarette. "The risk is frankly what makes him do it. My friend has wrestled the man-eating crocodile, survived the attack of the giant grizzly, fought off the jaws of the great white shark. He does this for a living, you see. He's quite well-known. Perhaps you've heard of him—his name is Wally Shluffmuffin."

"I don't care how well-known he is," said Sledge. "The name means nothing to me, and your friend is a fool. He wouldn't last sixty seconds with this creature."

"I, on the other hand, believe he *would* last sixty seconds," said The Jackal, with a grim smile. "I plan to videotape him from the other side of the glass. I already have a deal to sell the tape to a big TV reality show. My TV people will pay the same whether he lives or dies. Frankly, they'll pay *more* if he dies. I can sign a legal paper absolving you and the aquarium of all responsibility. I can make this venture very much worth your while."

"You don't say."

"I *do* say."

"How *much* worth my while?"

The Jackal smiled again, a different sort of smile. "*Very* much worth your while." He opened the black leather suitcase he'd been carrying. It was filled with bricks of newly minted hundred-dollar bills, Benjamin Franklin with pursed lips staring disapprovingly out from every one of them.

Sledge didn't react to the contents of the open suitcase for the longest time. Then, at last, he spoke.

"Midnight next Thursday," he said. "A back door will be left unlocked so you and your friend may come in unobserved. Your friend will enter the tank of the giant octopus and remain there for precisely six minutes. He will be permitted no scuba or other underwater breathing apparatus, no speargun or knife, no weapon of any kind. If he survives, you will both exit the aquarium as soon as the six minutes are up. If he does not survive—which he won't—the creature will ingest all traces of him and you will exit immediately. I will sign no papers. We have never spoken of this matter or anything else. I have forgotten your friend's name and I do not wish to know yours. We have never met."

Sledge grabbed the handle of the suitcase. His hand was seriously deformed. It looked as though it had no bones. It looked less like a hand than a tentacle with a double row of suckers.

CHAPTER 2

Mutants Do Seem to Lack the Common Courtesies

"Wally Shluffmuffin will die next Thursday at midnight," said Hedy Mandible.

"How do you know that?" asked the Ont Queen.

"I have The Jackal's word of honor on it," said Hedy.

"Assassins have no honor," said the queen.

"This one seems to feel he has a reputation to protect," said Hedy.

"Well, we hope you are right," said the Ont Queen. "If not, *your* reputation will suffer as well."

The whale-sized Ont Queen reclined on her ninety-foot-long royal sofa. She was clad in canvas camouflage fatigues that had been pieced together from numerous army tents. Stuck between her enormous mandibles was a large cigar.

The royal sofa was made of something purple and shiny, and it stood in the middle of an immense cavern. Redwood-sized stalagmites sprouted from the floor. Stalactites of equal size hung from the ceiling. Tall black wrought-iron candelabra held a thousand lit candles. The domed cavern itself was entirely plated in gold. Even the stalagmites and stalactites had been gold-plated, and they reflected the flames of the thousand flickering candles. The cave was damp. There was an odd coppery smell in the air.

Next to the queen was Hedy Mandible, a six-foot-tall ont who wore a partial mask covering one side of her disfigured face.

The chief worker ont entered.

"Mother of mothers, queen of all onts in the state of Ohio," said the chief worker ont, "is this a good time to talk with Hedy?"

The Ont Queen raised her claw and motioned for the chief worker ont to approach her throne.

"Proceed," said the queen.

"Thank you, My Queen," said the chief worker ont. "Hedy, have you seen the babies lately?"

"I visited the nursery a few weeks ago," said Hedy.

"Then you're aware of . . . the problem?" asked the chief worker ont.

"I'm aware that the human snot we've been feeding the babies has caused some unforeseen changes," said Hedy carefully.

"Mutations," said the chief worker ont. "Let's be frank about what these changes are—mutations. The human DNA in the snot has caused some of the babies to mutate into alarming, half-ont, half-human monsters who—"

"Monsters?" shouted the queen. "Our babies are most certainly not monsters! How dare you refer to our babies as monsters?"

The chief worker ont fell to the stone floor in front of the queen. She pressed her head to the cold surface and stretched her arms out in front of her.

"Forgive me, My Queen," said the chief worker ont. "I certainly meant no disrespect."

"Arise," said the queen in a voice not flowing with forgiveness.

"Thank you, My Queen," said the chief worker ont. "May I be allowed to bring in one of the children to show you what I'm talking about?"

The Ont Queen nodded.

The chief worker ont motioned to someone standing just outside. A moment later another worker came in, leading something unpleasant. The unpleasant thing was nearly three feet tall. It walked on two of its six legs, and its face looked half human and half ont. It had large compound eyes, feelers growing out of its forehead, a pair of mandibles that looked like pliers turned sideways, and its face was covered by human flesh.

The queen and Hedy both inhaled sharply at the sight.

"My Queen, may I present Betsy," said the chief worker ont. "Betsy, what do you say to your queen?"

"Hi, Queenie," said Betsy.

The Ont Queen recoiled.

"Betsy, that is *not* how you've been taught to speak to your queen!" said the chief worker ont.

"Should I have said Fatso?" asked Betsy.

"That will be *all,* young lady!" said the chief. She nodded to the worker who'd brought the mutant in. Betsy was whisked out of the throne room.

"I am so sorry, Your Highness," said the chief worker ont. "I should have warned you. I'm afraid *all* of the mutants are pretty much like that."

"What do you intend to do about it?" asked the queen.

"I thought that Hedy . . . I thought perhaps Hedy could get the Shluffmuffin girl in here to train the mutants. To civilize them a bit. I've heard that Hedy controls the Shluffmuffin girl by posthypnotic suggestion. Is that true?"

"So what?" said Hedy.

"Well, I've found that the mutants seem to have great interest in human girls of that age."

"Are the mutants all as rude and unruly as the one you brought me?" asked the queen.

"Your Highness, I fear that some are worse," said the chief worker ont.

"And what if the mutants refuse to learn from the Shluffmuffin girl?" asked the queen. "What if, say, they should cause her extreme physical harm?"

"We are prepared to take such a risk," said the chief worker ont.

"I have no problem with that," said Hedy.

"Very well then," said the queen. "Hedy, have Cheyenne Shluffmuffin brought in to begin the training of the mutants."

CHAPTER 3

Two Calls from a Concerned Citizen

When the phone began ringing, Shirley Spydelle was in the middle of making a complicated silk comforter. The enormous spider squeezed one last long strand of silk out of the spinnerets on her abdomen, then ambled over to the phone in a leisurely fashion, picked up the receiver in one of her many hands, and spoke. "Hello?"

"Hi, Shirl," said a voice. "It's me, Hortense Jolly, at the Jolly Days Orphanage. Howya doing?"

"Fine, thank you, Miss Jolly," said Shirley with little warmth.

"Shirl, you remember when we talked last, when poor Cheyenne was so ill, I asked you, seeing as how you and Professor Spydelle seem to have adopted her and Wally, to please drop me a check in the mail for the twelve-hundred-dollar adoption fee? Well, funny thing is, I haven't received it. Did you send it by certified mail, Shirl, because if you did, it should have come by now. I do hope you sent it by certified mail. When did you actually drop it in the mail, Shirl?"

"I'm afraid I never mailed you a check, Miss Jolly," said Shirley. She cleaned and buffed a spinneret.

"Aha," said Hortense. "Well, that explains it, doesn't it? I think you'll recall how fair I was, Shirl, how I bent over backwards to be fair, how I said—in the event that poor little Cheyenne died—I would gladly refund half the adoption fee, no questions asked? Do you recall my saying that?"

"I do," said Shirley, "but the thing is—"

"So what do I get for my generosity, Shirl, what do I get, will you tell me that?"

"Miss Jolly, I'm afraid our circumstances have changed," said Shirley. "The children have decided not to let us adopt them after all. They've decided to return to their father. So for us to send you an adoption fee would no longer be appropriate."

"You're saying the children now wish to be in the custody of their father, Mr. Sheldon Shluffmuffin, the vampire gentleman I met at your house?"

"That's correct," said Shirley. She wondered what she might fix for dinner. Maybe a nice *veau tarantelle*—the classic veal dish she'd been taught to prepare by tarantula friends in Florida, the center injected with flesh-dissolving saliva and turned to crimson jelly.

"Let me ask you a frank question, Shirl," said Hortense. "Do you think *he'd* be willing to pay me that adoption fee?"

"Well, I can't speak for Mr. Shluffmuffin," said Shirley, deciding against the *tarantelle,* "but my guess would be, seeing as how he's already their father, he might not think it necessary to pay you a fee to adopt his own children."

"Uh-huh. I see what you're saying," said

Hortense. "All righty then, nice talking to you, Shirl. My best to the professor."

Hortense opened the door to the broom closet, reached up to a high shelf, and took down the battered Cincinnati White Pages directory. The cover was ripped and frayed, and the orphans had scrawled unpleasant graffiti all over it. The truth was, Hortense Jolly didn't much care for children. How ironic that she, who'd never wanted any of her own, had ended up playing orphanage mom to three dozen of the little buggers.

She went through the listings of city agencies at the front of the directory and located the number she was looking for, then dialed.

"Child Welfare Bureau, good morning," said the voice.

"Oh, hello," said Hortense. "I'm calling as a concerned citizen to report two children living in unsafe conditions in the Greater Cincinnati Area. May I tell you their names and address?"

"To whom am I speaking?" asked the voice.

"A concerned citizen," said Hortense.

"Can you tell me your name, concerned citizen?" asked the voice.

"Do you want the names of these poor children who are living in unsafe conditions or don't you?" said Hortense.

"Go ahead," said the voice.

"Their names are Wally and Cheyenne Shluffmuffin," said Hortense. "A male and a female. They're ten years old, and they're currently residing at the home of Edgar and Shirley Spydelle in Dripping Fang Forest. How soon can you send someone over to investigate this case?"

There was a crash behind Hortense, somewhere downstairs, followed by kids screaming.

"What sort of unsafe conditions are these children living in?" asked the voice on the phone.

"The worst," said Hortense.

There was more screaming downstairs and another crash.

"Can you be any more specific than 'the worst'?" asked the voice.

"Okay," said Hortense. "These children are being forced to live in a house crawling with giant spiders and vampires."

"Giant what did you say?"

"Spiders and vampires!" shouted Hortense. "Is that specific enough for you?"

CHAPTER 4

Wally Is in Over His Head

ater.

Water in his ears. Water in his eyes. Water in his nose.

Wally's lungs still held enough air for maybe another ten or fifteen seconds of life, so long as he didn't let the air out and wasn't forced to breathe the water that pressed in on him from every angle.

His pulse was pounding in his ears. His chest was nearly bursting. On his wrist was a large black watch, its sweep–second hand measuring out his last few seconds of life on Earth.

Was the great white shark out of sight in the deep green water below him, its dead black eyes focusing in on him, its triple rows of triangular white teeth and obscene pink gums ready to chomp him in half? Was the school of flapping piranhas lurking somewhere behind him, every mouth a miniature buzz saw, preparing to engulf him in a bloody feeding frenzy? Had the yellow submersible with its crew of three terrified marine biologists dropped out of sight beneath him, the victim of a voracious sixty-foot-long giant squid that only he, the great Wally Shluffmuffin, could possibly save?

Then, quite unexpectedly, from somewhere there came a loud knocking sound and a faint echoing voice: "Wally, when are you going to be *done* in there? Other people need to use this bathroom, too, you know!"

Wally's head broke the surface of the warm water, his lungs screaming for air. Chest heaving, he hungrily gulped precious oxygen.

"I'm taking a *bath,* Cheyenne, okay?" he shouted. "It takes *time* to take a bath!"

"But you've been in that tub an *hour* already," called his ten-year-old twin sister. "Baths don't need to take a whole hour. Don't tell me you're in there playing with that new waterproof watch Dad bought you?"

"And what if I am?" Wally asked. "If you don't test these things, then one day when you really need them—when your very *life* depends on them—you find out that you can't depend on them because your sister was too selfish to let you test them and then you *die*. Is that what you want to happen to me, Cheyenne? Do you want me to die because I'm wearing a waterproof watch that you refused to let me test?"

CHAPTER 5

Can the Dead Become Truly Responsible Parents?

The social worker couldn't see chairs or a sofa in the Spydelles' living room, so she sat down on one of the hammocks and took out her clipboard. Vampire Dad sat on another hammock. There was no support for the woman's back, and she was forced to sit in an undignified and unbusinesslike position.

"So, Mr. Shluffmuffin," said the social worker, "the Child Welfare Bureau has received a report that one Walter Shluffmuffin, age ten, a male, and one Cheyenne Shluffmuffin, age ten, a female, are living here under substandard conditions."

"I don't know who would have told you

that," said Dad. "I've shown you their bedroom. You've seen the rest of the house. Would you call these conditions substandard?"

Instead of answering Dad's question, the social worker asked another. "What school do these children currently attend?"

"Right now, none," said Dad.

"Right now . . . children do not . . . attend school," mumbled the social worker, scribbling on her clipboard. "Sir, are you aware that the City of Cincinnati requires all children age sixteen and under to attend school?"

"Well," said Dad, "the Jolly Days Orphanage where they were living before had been homeschooling them."

"They were living in an orphanage?" asked the social worker.

"Yes, and then the Mandible sisters took them home for a trial adoption."

"I see," said the social worker. "But they are at present living neither at the orphanage nor with the adoptive parents?"

"That's right," said Dad.

The social worker frowned, bending over her clipboard in her undignified position on the hammock, and scribbled again, mumbling, "No longer . . . living at orphanage . . . nor with adoptive . . . parents."

"Why are they no longer living with the Mandible sisters?" asked the social worker.

"They ran away."

"Because they were mistreated?" asked the social worker, pen poised.

"No, because they discovered the Mandible sisters were giant ants."

"No longer . . . living with . . . Mandible sisters," mumbled the social worker, scribbling again, "because discovered . . . they were giant . . . Sir, you're spelling that A-U-N-T-S?"

"No, A-N-T-S."

"I see." The social worker looked like she was going to ask a follow-up question, then changed her mind. "I'm not exactly clear why these children were living at an orphanage to begin with," she said.

"Because for a period of time they were orphans," said Dad.

"In what sense were they orphans?" asked the social worker.

"In the sense that my wife and I were dead," said Dad.

"Excuse me?" said the social worker. She sensed that this line of questioning had just taken a bad turn.

"My wife, Sharon, was killed by a gang of crazed bunnies in a petting zoo," said Dad. "I myself drowned in a Porta Potti."

The social worker nodded slowly, then looked down at her clipboard. "Wife killed by . . . crazed bunnies," she muttered, scribbling. "Husband . . ." She looked up. "Sir, you're saying you died in a Porta Potti?"

"That's correct," said Dad.

"And then you were . . . brought back to life?" asked the social worker.

"Well, in a manner of speaking, yes," said Dad.

"Husband died in . . . Porta Potti," mumbled the social worker, continuing to scribble, "then . . . brought back . . . to life. Sir, how many minutes after you drowned in the Porta Potti were you brought back to life?"

"Oh, it wasn't a matter of minutes," said Dad. "It took more like three years."

The social worker stared at Dad.

"Okay, sir," said the social worker, trying in vain to sit up straight in the hammock. "I just want to make sure we're both on the same page here. So what you're telling me is that you drowned in a Porta Potti, and you were brought back to life . . . three years later?"

"About three years, right," said Dad. "Maybe a tad more. First I became a zombie, and then Professor Spydelle gave me his Elixir of Life, but it turned me into a . . . You could just put down three years if you like."

The social worker lost her balance at last and toppled over backward on the hammock.

"And despite being . . . *not alive* for those three years, sir," she said, sitting up again, unsteadily, trying to preserve her dignity, "you're now . . . perfectly all right?"

"When you say 'perfectly all right . . . ,'" said Dad, "Well, I don't know if I'd describe it that way exactly."

"You have some health problems as a result of being *unalive* for that period of time, sir?" said the social worker, bending over and scribbling again.

"In a manner of speaking, yes."

"And what would those be?" asked the social worker.

"Well, you know, there's the problem with my pulse and all."

"Has . . . problems with . . . pulse," she muttered, scribbling. "Do you have a rapid pulse, sir?"

"Not exactly rapid, no," said Dad. "It's actually more that I don't *have* a pulse."

"I see." She wrote carefully, mumbling, "Does not . . . have . . . a pulse."

The social worker looked like she wanted to ask a follow-up question; then she thought better of it. She consulted her clipboard.

"Tell me, Mr. Shluffmuffin, where are you currently employed?"

"I am not currently employed," said Dad.

"Then how will you support these children?" she said.

"Well, I intend to get a job."

"Do you have any occupational skills?" asked the social worker.

"Oh yes," said Dad. "I was an orthodontist before my, um, accident. But when I became a zombie, I found it hard to resume my practice."

The social worker put away her clipboard abruptly and managed to extract herself from the hammock and stand up.

"Mr. Shluffmuffin, I am giving you two weeks to enroll these children in school and to provide me with proof of your employment. Unless I have both of these things in two weeks' time, I will order that the children must be returned to the orphanage."

She left.

Wally and Cheyenne crept in. They'd been listening from their bedroom.

"Well, that didn't go terribly well, did it?" asked Dad.

"Oh, it could have been lots worse," said Cheyenne. She sneezed.

"Dad, maybe you gave her a little too much information," said Wally.

"What do you mean?" asked Dad.

"I mean maybe she didn't need to know all that stuff about your being dead and a zombie and all," said Wally.

"You don't want me to *lie,* do you?" Dad asked.

"No," said Wally. "But maybe you don't have to tell people more than they can handle."

"I guess you're right," said Dad. "Well, I'd better look into getting a job. And we'd better find a school for you two if we don't want the Child Welfare Bureau to send you back to the Jolly Days Orphanage."

CHAPTER 6

Meet the Mutants

Dark clouds scudded across a bloated yellow moon. Somewhere a wolf howled, and the pack responded with chilling mournful cries.

Cheyenne stirred in her sleep and then jolted awake. A dark shadow fell across the window of the ground-floor bedroom that she and Wally shared. Wally snored on, but Cheyenne sat up in bed.

Someone or something was outside the window. Now it held up a huge white cardboard sign printed with thick black letters. Cheyenne leaned forward and strained to see the words. She could barely make them out: WOULD YOU LIKE TO MEET THE BABIES?

Cheyenne didn't know what this meant; yet the words seemed strangely familiar. They imprinted themselves on her pupils, then sank deep into her brain, deep into her subconscious. With a little of sigh of resignation, she slipped into a light trance. She knew what she had to do.

Dressing quietly so as not to wake up her sleeping brother, Cheyenne walked zombielike out of the bedroom and out of the house into the night. Just past the door, the dark shape approached her. Taking her gently but firmly by the arm, it guided her into the misty woods, the yellow moon lighting their way.

"Your Highness," said Hedy, "Cheyenne has arrived."

"Bring her to us," said the Ont Queen.

Hedy motioned to someone, and Cheyenne was led into the throne room. Cheyenne seemed dazed by the thousand flickering candles reflecting off the gold stalactites and stalagmites. The smell of melting wax was not unpleasant.

"Good evening, dear," said Hedy. "It's good to see you again."

Cheyenne stared blankly ahead. She sneezed but did not reply.

"Can she hear you?" asked the Ont Queen.

"Oh yes, Your Highness," said Hedy. "She hears every word, although she will remember nothing. Cheyenne, dear, I have had you brought here tonight for a special purpose. I would like you to help us with the babies."

"The babies . . . ," Cheyenne repeated. She blew her nose.

"We are having a problem with some of the babies," said Hedy. "The ones who've been fed human snot have mutated. They look part human, but their behavior is not acceptable for either onts or humans. I would like you to teach them proper behavior. Proper manners. Proper respect for their elders. Do you think you can do that for me, dear?"

"Yes," said Cheyenne.

"Yes, *Ont Hedy.*"

"Yes, Ont Hedy," said Cheyenne.

"Excellent," said Hedy. "As usual when you come here, you will remember nothing once you leave. And now, let's go and meet the babies, dear. Come with me."

Hedy took Cheyenne by the hand and led her out of the throne room.

Hedy and Cheyenne entered a small classroom. Two dozen chair-desks faced a large teacher's desk at the front of the room. About twenty mutant ont children were screaming at one another, throwing chalk and blackboard erasers, and fighting as Hedy and Cheyenne came in.

"Quiet, children! Quiet!" Hedy shouted. The mutant children paid her no attention.

Hedy emitted a high, piercing, shrieking sound that seemed to hurt their ears, because they clapped their hands to their heads and stopped making noise.

"That's better," said Hedy. "Children, I'd like you to meet Cheyenne Shluffmuffin. I've asked her to come here and teach you some things I think you need to learn."

"*Shluffmuffin* is a stupid name," said one of the children.

"She's a human," said another.

"That's right," said Hedy.

"She's ugly," said the child called Betsy.

"She thinks you're ugly, dear," said Hedy.

Cheyenne seemed to be thinking this over. She blew her nose again.

"I don't think *she's* ugly," said Cheyenne slowly.

"That's because I'm *not,*" said Betsy. "But *you* sure are."

Cheyenne turned to face the mutant girl.

"Who cares . . . what you think?" said Cheyenne.

"Why don't you care?" Betsy asked.

"Because . . . you aren't anybody I . . . know or like," said Cheyenne. "Why should I . . . care what you think about me?"

"Children," said Hedy, "I didn't ask Cheyenne to come here so you could insult her. I asked her to come here so she could teach you things that could help you when you start meeting other humans."

"What could you teach us about humans?" asked one of the children.

Cheyenne seemed to be thinking this over. "What would you *like* me to teach you about humans?" she asked.

"The most exciting way to kill them," said Betsy.

CHAPTER 7

Cheyenne, Cheyenne, Where Have You Been? I've Been to the Ont Cave to Visit the Queen.

Later, when Cheyenne crept back into the bedroom, Wally sat up in bed.

The sky had begun to lighten in the east. Owls were the only birds awake, endlessly repeating their single senseless question: *Who? Who? Who?*

"Where have you been?" Wally asked.

"Huh?" said Cheyenne, startled.

"Where have you been?" Wally repeated.

"I don't know," she said. "The bathroom, I think."

"The bathroom? You were gone for *hours,* Cheyenne."

"That's impossible," she said. "Are you sure?"

"Absolutely," said Wally. "I woke up about one A.M. Now it's almost five."

Cheyenne sat down on her bed.

"I don't know where I've been," she said. She sighed and blew her nose. "I don't know what's happening to me."

"I think the onts have given you some kind of posthypnotic suggestion, Cheyenne. I'm almost sure of it," said Wally. "The next time they send for you, I'm coming, too."

"Oh no, Wally," she said. "It's too dangerous. If they see you, they'll kill you."

"I've thought of a way around that," said Wally. "If my plan works, even if they see me, they might become very friendly."

When Wally walked into Edgar's study before breakfast, he found the professor at his desk, staring into space. Beakers filled with beautiful red, blue, and purple liquids bubbled merrily over Bunsen burners. There was a delicate flowery smell in the air, not unlike orange blossoms.

"Hi, Professor," said Wally. "How's it going?"

Edgar turned around and looked at him.

"Do you really wish to know how it's going, old boy," asked Edgar in his charming British accent, "or are you simply making small talk?"

"What?" said Wally.

"I say, it's difficult to imagine that you actually want to know how it's going," said Edgar, "given your behavior on the bridge the other day."

"Uh . . . what are you talking about?" Wally asked.

"On the bridge when we were trying to prevent your father from falling to his death?" said Edgar. "A ludicrous notion, I hasten to add, since vampires are already dead, but I do seem to recall you and your sister telling him that you love him more than you love me and Shirley."

"Oh, is *that* what this is about?" asked Wally.

"Did you tell him that or didn't you?" Edgar asked.

"Well, sure, Professor. I mean, he's my *dad*."

"And who am *I*, then," said Edgar, "some poor wretch you asked to adopt you, only to be tossed aside like an old shoe?"

Wally closed his eyes. What are you supposed to do when grown-ups act like children?

"Professor, I'm sorry if we hurt your feelings," said Wally, "but if you'll remember, the main reason we asked you to adopt us was that Shirley was so hot to have kids, we thought if we didn't, she'd want to have babies with you, and then she'd have to . . . you know."

"Kill me and eat me," said Edgar. "Go ahead and say it. That's what spiders do, you see, it's nothing personal."

"Yeah," said Wally, "so we were trying to save your life."

"And you don't even love us one little bit, do you?" said Edgar, busying himself among his beakers.

"Hey, no, that's not true, Professor," said Wally. "We *do* love you guys, we love you a lot, only . . ."

"Only not as much as you love your father," said Edgar. "Fine. I'm glad we've settled *that.* Now, what did you come in here to ask me, since it obviously wasn't to find out how things were going?"

"Well, okay, here's the thing," said Wally. "I want to go back to the Ont Queen's cave, okay? And I thought maybe you could put together something that would put the guards to sleep. Some kind of pheromone thing, since ants are so sensitive to smells."

"Oh, really?" said Edgar. He turned off two of the Bunsen burners and stirred the liquid in each beaker with a long glass rod. The orange-blossom smell grew stronger. "Well, if you're such an expert on ant sensitivity, then what kind of pheromone did you have in mind?"

"I don't think I'm an expert," said Wally, "but I do read encyclopedias a lot. I thought maybe you could put together some hydrocarbons or something."

"Oh, you did, did you?" said Edgar, looking away from Wally. "Well, since you know so much about it, why don't you just do it your-self? Why do you even need me?"

"Professor," said Wally, "give me a break here, would you? Look, I'm really sorry we hurt your feelings, I swear. And I can't put together hydrocarbons to make pheromones by myself because I don't know how. I'm just a kid. But you're a professor and you know how to do these things. If you could put something together to help me, I'd sure appreciate it."

Edgar kept looking away from Wally. Finally he sighed.

"Very well," he said. "I shall see what I can come up with."

CHAPTER 8

We Here at DFFCDS Do Not Tolerate the Intolerant

"I still don't see why we have to go to school," said Wally. "We didn't have to go to school when we were at Jolly Days. I learned more from studying the encyclopedia than I ever would going to school."

It was a crisp, cool morning, and Vampire Dad and the twins were walking through woods that smelled like a huge Christmas tree lot.

"Well, maybe Hortense Jolly had some kind of arrangement with the authorities," said Dad. "In any case, you both have to be registered in a school and I have to get a job, or they'll take you guys away from me and send you back to Jolly Days."

"I'd do anything not to go back *there* again," said Wally.

"Oh, Wally, Jolly Days wasn't that bad," said Cheyenne. She sneezed and blew her nose.

"Really?" said Wally. "You mean you didn't mind scrubbing floors and toilets with boiling water and Lysol six hours a day? Or sleeping on a bare mattress on the floor with rats and cockroaches?"

"If we hadn't spent so long scrubbing," said Cheyenne, "it never would have been so clean. And you can't tell me those cockroach races weren't fun."

The letters on the sign outside the rustic little building ahead of them were made of twigs: THE DRIPPING FANG FOREST COUNTRY DAY SCHOOL.

"Here we are, kids," said Dad.

"Is today our first day of class?" asked Cheyenne.

"Oh no," said Dad. "Today's just an interview with the headmaster. We don't even know if they'll accept you."

They entered the rustic building. A heavy

wooden door had the word HEADMASTER on it, also spelled out in twigs. Dad opened it and they walked in.

"May I help you?" asked a woman behind a reception desk. She had glasses trimmed in rhinestones hanging from a thick black ribbon around her neck. Her ears were long and floppy. A troll.

"Hi," said Dad. "We're the Shluffmuffins. We had a nine o'clock appointment?"

"Ah yes," said the troll. "Good morning, Mr. Stuffmuffin."

"Actually, it's *Shluffmuffin,*" said Dad.

She got up, went to another door, knocked, opened the door, and stuck her head inside.

"The Stuffmuffins are here," she said, then turned back to Dad and the twins. "You may go right in."

They entered the headmaster's office. Behind a large desk made out of rough timber that had been smoothed and sanded and lacquered to a high gloss sat the headmaster. He was husky, with bushy eyebrows and a gruff face, an unremarkable man except for the impressive set of antlers that grew out of his head.

Wally and Cheyenne tried not to stare at the antlers. But it was impossible not to.

"Good morning, Mr. Stiffmitten," said the headmaster, rising and extending a meaty hand for Dad to shake.

"Shluffmuffin," said Dad. "Good to meet you, sir. And these are my children, Cheyenne and Wally."

The headmaster looked the twins up and down with a tightening frown.

"I'm afraid there's been a misunderstanding," said the headmaster. "I was told that the children were, ah—how shall I put this?—normal."

"Normal?" said Dad. "They *are* normal. *Quite* normal, I assure you."

"Yes, yes, of course they are," said the headmaster. "I didn't mean *normal.* I just meant that we at Dripping Fang Country Day do try to maintain a student body where the children are all, uh, very much . . . very much . . . What I'm trying to say is that we at DFFCDS have certain standards that . . ."

Cheyenne stifled a sneeze.

"You're trying to say you accept only certain

groups of children and not others?" said Dad, getting annoyed.

"No-no-no-no-no-no-*no,*" said the headmaster, raising both hands as if to ward off blows. "Oh *my,* no. That would be prejudice or discrimination. We at DFFCDS most certainly do not tolerate prejudice or discrimination. *Heavens,* no. What I'm saying is that we've just found, over the years, the way that we in the community here and that the children *themselves* have felt most comfortable is by being with those who are most *like* them. Most *similar* to them. And the great majority of our children do tend to come from fine old families that have lived here in the forest for many generations, that understand and share the same values and traditions, and that have many very special gifts or features that might otherwise distinguish them from . . . from . . ."

"Features?" said Dad, even more annoyed. "You mean features like these?" He bared his fangs, shrugged off his coat, and extended his leathery wings to their full width.

The headmaster stared at the wings. His eyebrows climbed his forehead, and then his features relaxed.

"I'm *so* glad you understand," he said. "And the children . . . ?" He glanced at Cheyenne and Wally.

"My children take after me in almost all respects," said Dad.

The headmaster sat back down behind his desk and composed his features into what he must have thought looked like a smile. "Well, Mr. Stuffmutton, I think your family will feel quite at home here at Dripping Fang Country Day."

CHAPTER 9

School Days, School Days, Dear Old Golden Ghoul Days

"I just don't see why we have to wear these stupid uniforms," said Wally.

"Oh, they're not that bad," said Cheyenne. "In fact, I kind of like them."

It was a few days later. Cheyenne and Wally were walking through the forest on their first day of school. The sun was hot. Small yellow butterflies flitted in front of them. Perky brown birds sang cheerful repetitive songs.

Cheyenne and Wally both wore white shirts and black blazers with a crest on the pocket that had the school insignia, which looked like an Old English shield with the letters *DFFCDS* intertwined with crossed swords, a snarling wolf's head, and a pine tree. Cheyenne wore a tan skirt, and Wally wore tan slacks and a tie in the school colors, purple and black.

"I also hate that headmaster," said Wally. "What a phony. He wasn't even going to take us till he saw Dad's wings."

"But then he got really nice," said Cheyenne, sneezing. "You can't blame him for being more comfortable with weird people like himself."

"Yes, I can," said Wally.

They entered the schoolhouse and stopped at the receptionist's desk.

"Which classroom are we in?" Cheyenne asked the troll.

"There's only one," said the troll, smiling. She pointed. "It's right through there."

There was a lot of noise coming out of the classroom.

The first thing Cheyenne and Wally noticed when they entered was that the other students seemed to be of many different ages and back-grounds, but all wore the school uniform. There were six wolf cubs, two trolls with red buzz cuts and floppy ears, a giant slug about three feet long, a young ghoul with saggy white cheeks and sharp yellow teeth, and a boy whose eyes were located at the ends of stalks.

Standing at a huge green blackboard was the teacher, a woman with a large birdlike beak where her nose and mouth could have been. Everyone stopped talking when Cheyenne and Wally walked in.

"Well, these must be our new students," said the teacher in a shrill, screechy voice, "Cheyenne and Wally Studmuppet. Welcome to our class, children."

"It's actually *Shluffmuffin,*" said Wally. "Hi."

"Hi," said Cheyenne, stifling a sneeze and blowing her nose. "It's really nice to be here."

"I'm your teacher, Mrs. McCaw," said the teacher. "You can have those two desks at the back of the room."

Cheyenne and Wally sat down. The other kids continued to stare at them.

"Children," said Mrs. McCaw, "you'll be interested to know that Cheyenne and Wally's father is a vampire, and their mother is . . . I'm sorry, children, what is your mother again?"

"Dead," said Wally.

"Oh yes, dead. Sorry," said Mrs. McCaw. "And is she still . . . with us?"

"No," said Cheyenne. "We buried her three years ago."

"Ah," said Mrs. McCaw, "what a pity. Well, Cheyenne and Wally, I'm glad you arrived. We were just about to start our lessons for today. This week we've been studying insects. Has either of you had any firsthand experience with insects, other than swatting them on your neck, I mean?"

Wally raised his hand. "Right now we're living with an enormous spider named Shirley Spydelle," he said.

"Thank you, Wally," said Mrs. McCaw. "I know Mrs. Spydelle. Of course, she's an *arachnid,* not an insect, isn't she?"

Cheyenne raised her hand. "Wally and I were

adopted by the Mandible sisters," she said. "They're giant ants."

"Yes, dear," said Mrs. McCaw, "we heard about that awful fire at Mandible House. When you were with the Mandibles, did you learn anything about ant culture that you'd like to share with the class?"

"Ants keep aphids the way humans keep cows," said Wally.

"Oh, heavens, I doubt *that,*" said Mrs. McCaw, with a superior smile.

Wally had not only read in the encyclopedia about ants keeping aphids like cattle, he'd actually seen this in the Ont Queen's cave, but he decided it wasn't worth arguing about. "Well, I could be wrong," he said.

"I should hope so," said Mrs. McCaw.

During morning recess in the school yard, the other kids gathered around Cheyenne and Wally and just stared at them.

"Is your father really a vampire?" asked one of the wolf kids.

"What of it?" said Wally.

"Does he bite you and suck your blood?" asked another wolf kid.

"Does *your* father suck *yours,* dog breath?" asked Wally.

"Who you calling dog breath, stinky feet?" asked the wolf kid, coming closer.

"I mean *you,* dog breath," said Wally, "but it doesn't smell like *any* of you owns a toothbrush."

The other wolf kids drew closer as well.

"You wouldn't be trying to insult us, would you?" asked one of them.

"Nope," said Wally, "I did it *without* trying." He began a low growl in his throat, which made the wolf kids uneasy.

"Are you and your sister vampires, too?" asked a troll kid.

"Maybe we are and maybe we aren't," said Cheyenne. "Want to find out the hard way?"

Wally flashed her an admiring look.

"What's *that* supposed to mean?" asked the troll kid.

"Keep bugging us and you'll find out," said Cheyenne. Then *she* growled.

The wolf cubs backed away.

"You guys are freaks," said the boy with eyes at the ends of stalks.

"Then I guess we came to the right school, huh?" said Wally.

CHAPTER 10

What Has Three Hearts, Blue Blood, and Is Red All Over?

The more one learns about the octopus, the more it seems to be a creature from an alien planet.

The octopus has three hearts that pump blue blood. It has a huge pouch-shaped head that holds all its internal organs and a mouth. It has no ears and can't hear, but it has two highly developed eyes that can swivel to see in all directions. It has eight powerful tentacles, or arms, the undersides of which are each equipped with 240 suction cups in double rows. As the tentacles wrap desperately struggling prey in a death hug, the suction cups fasten onto the prey, smelling and tasting it before bringing it to the mouth, located at the center of the tentacles.

Inside the mouth is a sharp parrotlike beak. The beak is used to bite prey and inject it with paralyzing, flesh-dissolving saliva before tearing it to pieces. If a tentacle is bitten or torn off in a struggle, the octopus will grow a new one. Because it has neither bones nor shell, the octopus can compress itself to about a thirtieth of its width and squeeze through narrow openings.

The octopus is a master of disguise. By contracting skin cells filled with pigment, an octopus can completely change both its color and texture to match its background in only half a second. It will also turn white with fear or red with rage. The octopus hunts at night. It escapes predators by sucking in seawater and then pumping it out through a funnel in its head, propelling itself backward. It may also squirt a cloud of ink to hide itself from attack.

Octopuses are curious and quite intelligent. They've climbed aboard fishing boats and opened

compartments full of crabs. They've unscrewed the tops of glass jars to get at shellfish inside.

The largest known species is the North Pacific giant octopus, found off the Pacific Coast from Alaska to California. One specimen reported in 1957 was thirty feet in diameter and weighed six hundred pounds.

The octopus in the tank in front of The Jackal at the Hotchkiss Aquarium weighed well over four hundred pounds. Its rubbery-looking tentacles were at least fifteen feet long, and they restlessly coiled and uncoiled like a nest of writhing boa constrictors. The animal was reddish brown, and its large lidded eyes, which had been closed for quite some time, had opened and now swiveled in The Jackal's direction, studying him with undisguised interest.

The Jackal shuddered, glad it would be Wally Shluffmuffin and not he who'd soon be in with the giant octopod. He walked through a door marked EMPLOYEES ONLY and surveyed the tank from the rear.

It was about fifty feet long and maybe twenty feet wide and no more than eight feet deep. There was a rocky enclosure on the bottom that the animal could use as a den. The back wall had been painted to look like an underwater view of the ocean.

Would it be more amusing if Wally were conscious when he hit the water?

CHAPTER 11

Most Orthodontists Tend Not to Have Such a Pronounced Overbite

The woman with the big smile and the staggeringly sweet perfume peered at her note card, then got up to shake hands.

"So, Mr. . . . Sluffmuffin is it?" she said. "Welcome to Headhunters Employment Agency. How can we help you today?"

"Actually," said Dad, "it's *Shluffmuffin. Dr.* Shluffmuffin. And I need to find a job pretty quickly, or my kids will have to go back to the orphanage." Uh-oh, he sensed that he'd already done what Wally had advised him not to—tell more than people really needed to know.

"You're a *doctor*?" said the woman. Her smile expanded to fill the entire room. "A surgeon, a cardiologist, an internist, or . . . ?"

"An orthodontist," said Dad.

"Ah," said the woman, her smile deflating. She sat back down again. "Why would you be looking for a job? Most doctors and dentists I know already have a practice."

"Well, I've been . . . out of the business for a few years," said Dad, "and I'm trying to get back in now."

"I see," said the woman. "So you're coming to us not to start up your own practice again but to find a position with another orthodontist until you manage to build up your own list of patients?"

"Something like that, yes," said Dad.

The woman nodded. Then she frowned and leaned forward. "Excuse me for asking this, Dr. Shluffmuffin," she said, "but I couldn't help noticing your teeth. The upper ones seem to be a tad, um, long at the corners there. This wouldn't be an example of your own work, would it?"

"Oh, no-no-no," said Dad, trying quickly to tuck his lips over his fangs. "That's just something that happened when I became a vam— That's just something that happened. They just started growing one day, and I haven't had a chance yet to . . . file them down or anything."

"I see."

There was an uncomfortable pause.

"Are you saying that maybe I should . . . have that taken care of before applying for a job with an orthodontist?"

"I'm thinking that might really be the best idea," said the woman.

"Okay," said Dad. "And after I do that, I can come right back here?"

"Absolutely."

The woman gave him a big smile, although not nearly as big as when she'd thought he might be a surgeon, a cardiologist, or an internist.

Back at the Spydelles', Dad went into the kitchen, opened the tool drawer, and rummaged around in it, but he couldn't find a file. He found a piece of sandpaper and started rubbing it against the point on one of his fangs. Sandpaper wasn't going to do the trick, he realized. What he needed was a file.

Dad walked out to the garage and opened the battered steel toolbox. There were lots of rusty hammers and screwdrivers inside but no files. He looked around the garage. In the corner was a large electric belt sander. Not quite the right tool for the job, but Dad didn't want to go out and buy dental tools, and he couldn't find a file....

He shrugged and turned on the machine. The sander came to life with a jolt and a whine. The sanding belt began whirring across the steel table. Dad squatted down till his face was level with the whirring belt. Carefully, he opened his jaws as wide as he could and lowered his face until the tips of his fangs met the belt.

Zzzzzzzzzzzt. Zzzzzzzzzzzt. The sander sent a funny tingly feeling through Dad's bones, but it did seem to be working. The tips of his fangs were no longer sharp. *Zzzzzzzzzzzt. Zzzzzzzzzzzt.* Now his fangs were so dull they wouldn't tear wet bread. *Hey,* he thought, *the belt sander—an exciting new breakthrough in cut-rate orthodontistry.*

CHAPTER 12

Mastering the Subtle Art of Job Interviews

"Do come in, please, Mr. . . . Fluffmuffin, is it?"

"*Shluffmuffin,*" said Dad. "Thanks."

The gray-haired woman with the round steel-rimmed glasses ushered him into her tiny office. Her hair was pulled so tightly into a bun at the top of her head that her eyes were popping.

"So you're applying for the position as dental assistant?" she said.

"That's right."

"Good," said the pop-eyed woman. "And you . . ." She leaned forward across the desk. "Excuse me for saying this, but your canine teeth are quite pronounced. Have you thought of having corrective orthodontistry?"

"I have," said Dad, "but it didn't seem to help."

"You've actually tried to have the condition corrected?"

"Yes," said Dad, "but it didn't take."

"Who did the work, if you don't mind my asking?"

"Well," said Dad, "I did it myself actually. I filed them down on a belt sander last night, but by morning they'd grown back. It was the darnedest thing." Uh-oh. Had he told her more than she needed to know?

"You're telling me you filed down your teeth on . . . a belt sander?" the pop-eyed woman asked, her eyes even more popped.

"Right."

"And . . . they grew back overnight, you say?"

"Well, not overnight exactly," said Dad. "It was more like a couple of weeks. And, come to think of it now, it wasn't a belt sander, it was . . . a dental sander kind of thing. I'm sure you've seen them—I have one in my garage."

The pop-eyed woman made a sound like a ringing telephone. *"Brrrinnng! Brrrinnng!"* Then she picked up the phone on her desk. "Hello," she said. "Yes. Oh, really? Well, thanks for telling me. Good-bye."

She put down the receiver. "I'm sorry, Mr. Muffstuffin," she said, "I've just been informed that the position of dental assistant has been filled."

"But there wasn't anybody on the other end when you picked up the phone," said Dad.

"Yes, there was."

"No, there wasn't," said Dad. "You made a noise like a ringing telephone, and then you had an imaginary conversation with yourself."

"No, I didn't."

"Yes, you did."

"Well, maybe I did," said the pop-eyed woman, "but the position has been filled, regardless. Good *day.*"

"Good afternoon, Mr. Snuffmuffin," said the skinny woman in the starched white lab coat.

Her nose was the size of a small banana. "You're here about the job of . . . ?"

"Dental janitor," said Dad. "And the name, by the way, is *Shluffmuffin.*"

The skinny woman led him into a very small room with two chairs. Clothes hooks on the wall held two white lab coats and a denim work shirt. The room was so tiny that when they sat down, Dad could barely avoid jamming his knees into hers. She made no mention of this, so he didn't, either. It was impolite to stare at her nose, but it was also unavoidable.

"You've had experience in cleaning dental workplaces, I understand?" said the banana-nosed woman.

"Why, yes," said Dad, smiling at the memory. "I kept an orthodontist's office clean for many years."

"Very well," she said. "Are you skilled in the use of the equipment?"

"The dental equipment?" said Dad, more pleasant memories flitting across his mental screen. "Of course."

"No, I meant the janitorial equipment."

"Oh, you meant the push broom, the mop and pail?" said Dad. "Yes, I've had extensive experience with those. In fact, I was a janitorial sciences major in college."

The banana-nosed woman fixed him with an icy stare.

"Was that supposed to be a joke?" she asked.

"Uh, yes," said Dad. "I'm sorry."

"If this is a joke to you, Mr. Slugmutton," said the banana-nosed woman, "perhaps you're the wrong man for the job. We take our work here very seriously."

"So do I, I assure you," said Dad. He had a sudden vision of Cheyenne and Wally, their arms outstretched, being dragged away from him by the social worker, and handed over to Hortense Jolly. "I promise that if you give me this job," said Dad, "I'll be so serious you will never even see me smile."

The banana-nosed woman's stare softened slightly.

"Well, all right then," she said. "I think we

can work together. You even look like you're the same size as the gentleman we had before. Would you mind trying his shirt on for size?"

"Oh, sure."

She reached up and lifted the denim shirt off a clothes hook.

Dad stood up and slipped off his jacket, his elbows smacking her in the nose, then began unbuttoning his shirt. He hoped she wouldn't ask about the small medicated adhesive patch on his shoulder that was numbing his thirst for human blood.

"Uh, excuse me," said the banana-nosed woman, staring at him. "You don't actually have . . . *wings* growing out of your back, do you?"

"Me?" said Dad.

"Yes, you."

"Well, maybe one or two," said Dad. "Why? Is that a problem for you?"

CHAPTER 13

No, I Don't Want to See Any of Your Stupid Babies

Cheyenne was having a nightmare. Hideous-looking children were tugging at her clothes, yanking at her arms, pulling her in opposite directions, demanding she feed and take care of them. There were too many of these children, and although Cheyenne *did* want to help them, she felt incapable and overwhelmed.

She snorted herself abruptly awake and lay in the dark for several minutes, trying to remember where she was. The dream had seemed so real. The hideous-looking children had seemed so familiar. Had she dreamed this dream before?

There was a soft scratching at the bedroom window. She sat up and looked. There was a dark shape outside the window. *I know what happens next,* she thought suddenly. *A sign—there'll be some kind of sign in the window, and then I'll be told to do something I don't want to do. Is this how alien abductions start? Am I being abducted by creatures from another planet? Are they outside now, weird little guys with huge heads, gray skin, and enormous black eyes?*

Sure enough, here came the sign. It said . . . Cheyenne leaned forward and squinted in the moonlight that was coming in through the window: WOULD YOU LIKE TO MEET THE BABIES?

Babies? What babies? She didn't know any babies. She didn't *want* to know any babies. She was far too young to have to worry about taking care of babies.

There was a tapping on the window.

No thanks, Cheyenne thought. *I don't want to see any of your stupid babies. I'm busy, I'm sleeping, maybe some other time. Good night.*

The tapping on the window grew more insistent. Although she had no intention of doing so, Cheyenne got slowly out of bed and stood silently staring at the window.

Wally stirred in his sleep, then woke up. He opened his eyes, saw Cheyenne standing beside her bed, and instantly knew what was happening. Cheyenne was being summoned to the Ont Queen's cave.

Should he snap her out of her trance, or should he pretend to be asleep and then follow her as he'd done before? If he woke her up now, he could prevent her from going. But if he followed her instead, he might be able to learn more about what the onts were making her do—and then maybe he could figure out how to stop them.

There was also a third choice, and he took it.

"Cheyenne," Wally whispered. "Wake up. Wake up, but pretend you're still asleep."

Cheyenne jolted awake.

"Sssshhh," Wally whispered. "I just woke you out of a trance, Cheyenne. The Ont Queen is sending for you again. If you can hear me, say

yes, but quietly. Pretend you're still in a trance. Can you hear me, Cheyenne?"

"Yesssss."

"Good," said Wally. "You've been to the Ont Queen's cave twice before in a trance. I want you to go *awake* this time. I want you to *fake* the trance. We could learn so much about what the onts are up to, and I'll come with you. I'll follow you from a distance. What do you say?"

"Yesssss."

"Good girl," said Wally. "Put on a sweater and go. Move slowly and act like you're half-asleep. Move like Dad moved when he was a zombie. Remember? I'll wait till you get a little ahead of me, and then I'll follow you. I know how to get to the Ont Queen's cave now, even if I lose you."

Cheyenne slowly picked up her sweater and put it on. She slowly put on her sneakers, too. Then, still slowly, zombielike, she walked out of the bedroom, the floorboards squeaking slightly.

As soon as Cheyenne left, Wally crept out of the room as well. But instead of following her to the front door, he turned and went into Edgar and Shirley's bedroom.

Wally heard the sounds of soft snoring. Edgar and Shirley were cuddled together in their silk pajamas in the center of a huge spiderweb that stretched the length of the bedroom. They looked so cozy, curled up tightly. Wally knew it was a terrible invasion of their privacy to be there, and he was nervous about waking them, but he felt he didn't have much choice.

"Edgar?" he whispered. "Edgar, it's me, Wally. Can I ask you something?"

Edgar muttered something unintelligible, then snapped into wakefulness.

"Huh? What? Whazzat?" he sputtered.

"Edgar, it's me, Wally. I'm sorry to bother you, but it's really important."

"Wally? What's the matter?" said Edgar. "Are you unwell? My word, what is the hour?"

"Edgar?" muttered Shirley sleepily. "What is it?"

"It's Wally," said Edgar. "He just awakened me."

"Are the children sick?" Shirley asked.

"No," said Wally, "we're not sick. I'm sorry to wake you guys, but I need help. The Ont Queen has sent for Cheyenne. I need to follow her, but I wondered if Edgar had a chance to make up those pheromones. I could sure use them at the cave to put the guards to sleep. Did you have a chance to make up those pheromones, Edgar?"

"I did," said Edgar. "Not that you could ever realize how much trouble I went to, and not that you care."

"I *do* realize, Edgar, and I *do* care," said Wally. "Honest, I think it's great."

"Well, not bloody likely, but if you go into my study, you'll find the pheromones in the blue spray bottle on my desk. A single spray should put several giant ants to sleep."

"Awesome," said Wally. "I really do appreciate this."

"Whatever," said Edgar.

"Do you want us to come with you, dear?" asked Shirley, carefully stretching out all her legs in turn. "We could get your father, too. We were pretty helpful at the fall of the House of Mandible, you know."

"I know you were," said Wally. "But I think Cheyenne and I would attract less attention in the ont colony if we went alone."

"Well then, do be careful," said Shirley.

By the time Wally found the blue spray bottle in Edgar's study and headed into the forest, Cheyenne and her black-clad escort were pretty far ahead of him. Wally could barely see them. The nearly full moon painted the woods in eerie blue-white light, making it much too bright to follow closely without being noticed, but Wally knew the route well enough by now that he could lag behind without getting lost.

A cool breeze rustled through the trees, carrying fragrances of pine and cedar. The night bugs—crickets and cicadas—made their tiny music as Wally crept quietly along the narrow paths. He heard the mournful howling of the man-eating wolves in the distance. Although he'd outbluffed the wolves more than once, he knew his luck wouldn't hold forever.

Twigs behind him snapped sharply. He froze. Was it the wolves? The giant slug? The freaks from Dripping Fang Country Day?

Wally could feel his heart hammering in his chest. *Please don't be something awful that I'll have to fight,* he thought. *I'm not a very good fighter.* He wished he *were* a good fighter, but about all he knew how to do was to punch somebody in the stomach.

"I know you're there," he said. "I should warn you that I'm armed. And my hands are registered as lethal weapons. Go on, make my day."

Pathetic, he thought. *How scary am I, quoting lines from old movies?*

There was no answer . . . and no movement from the direction of the snapped twigs.

The escort leading her through the woods, Cheyenne thought, was pretty creepy. The creature was dressed completely in black, its face covered by a wide black hat, and it never spoke a word. Well, maybe it was just shy.

Wally was right, she thought. Being awake and pretending to be in a trance was scary. *How sleepy should I act? Should I seem to have trouble standing up straight? Should I speak normally or like somebody who's half-asleep?* Was Wally right that she'd been to the Ont Queen's cave twice before in a trance? She didn't remember being there at all. It was as though it had never happened.

She stifled a sneeze and blew her nose. She could neither see nor hear Wally behind her. She didn't even know if he was there. She felt alone and very vulnerable. But whatever happened, it would probably be an experience she'd learn a lot from and later be glad she'd had.

I've been a complete idiot, thought Wally miserably. *How could I have asked my own sister to do something as dangerous as go back to the Ont Queen's cave in a pretend trance? How could she know how a person acts when they're in a trance? How could she possibly fool them? And what will they do to her when they find out she's faking? Is it too late to call this off, too late to abort the mission? Can I catch up with her, punch her escort in the stomach, and yell for Cheyenne to run for her life?*

Wally broke into a run. He tried not to make much noise, but his footfalls on the path echoed in the quiet forest.

Was that them, way up ahead? He couldn't be sure. He ran faster, his breath catching in his throat, his pulse pounding. Yes, it was. He could see them. He'd have to go slower so they wouldn't hear him coming. Then, when he was almost up to them . . .

Uh-oh. He recognized a rock formation ahead on the right. They were almost to the cave. It was too dangerous to change the plan now. The guards would hear the commotion and come out. They'd grab Cheyenne, and it would be terrible. It was too late to save her. He had blown it.

CHAPTER 14

Come On, Give a Bug a Hug

Two onts in camouflage fatigues materialized in front of Cheyenne and her escort. You could barely distinguish the onts from the trees in the dark, dappled forest.

"Halt!" said one. "Who goes there—friend or foe?"

"Cheyenne Shluffmuffin and a friend," said Cheyenne's escort. "She wants to meet the babies."

"She is expected," said the second ont, saluting smartly.

Wow, thought Cheyenne. *So the onts have soldiers. I wonder if I've seen all this before.*

The two soldier onts let Cheyenne and her escort pass into the mouth of the cave. As soon as they were out of sight, Wally boldly stepped from behind a tree.

"Halt!" said an ont guard. "Who goes there—friend or foe?"

"Foe," said Wally. He raised the professor's blue spray bottle and gave them two quick blasts. "Nighty-night, girls!"

The two guards seemed momentarily stunned. Then, instead of staggering about and falling to the ground, they staggered about and began giggling hysterically.

"Nighty-*night,* girls?" said one of them. "Nighty-*night,* girls? Is he cute or what?"

"Adorable!" said the other. "I always thought humans were disgusting, but this one is cute as a bug's ear! What's your name, honey?"

She moved toward Wally with her arms out for a hug. Wally backed away from her, confused. This wasn't supposed to be happening. The ont guards were supposed to be lying on the ground, fast asleep, not behaving like his grandma Gloria's friends.

"Give us a hug, dear," said the other, walking toward him with her arms out as well. "Ooh, he's so cute I could just eat him up!"

"I'm not really too big on hugs from people I don't know," said Wally, continuing to back away. *And especially not from giant ants.*

"Oh, come on, just a *tiny* hug," said the other guard. "It won't kill you."

"Thanks just the same," said Wally. "Maybe some other time."

He turned and began running into the tunnel, toward where Cheyenne and her escort had disappeared. But three ont workers were coming in his direction.

"Stop that boy!" yelled one of the guards. "He refuses to give hugs!"

"He refuses to give *what*?" asked the biggest of the three workers. She was the size of a Cincinnati Bengals fullback.

"Hugs!" shouted the first guard.

All three workers stopped, thoroughly confused. Wally gave them several blasts from his blue spray bottle. The workers staggered about, then began giggling hysterically.

"You won't give *hugs*?" said the one who looked like a fullback. "Not even to *us*? Not even the teensiest hugs in the whole wide world?" She and her friends giggled like she'd just uttered the funniest line ever.

It had been a big mistake to spray the workers. Fighting off giant onts who were trying to kill you was bad enough. Fighting off giant onts who were trying to hug you was way more than Wally could handle.

"Hugs!" echoed all the onts. "Hugs! Hugs! Hugs! Hugs! Hugs! Hugs! Hugs!" they chanted, closing in on him.

Wally turned and fled toward the cave entrance, sidestepping hug-crazed onts like a broken-field runner.

CHAPTER 15

Let's Make Cheyenne Do Something Gross and Disgusting

"Children," said Hedy, "I have brought Cheyenne back to help you understand more about humans."

They were once again in the mutants' classroom, the unruly little monsters squabbling among one another as usual.

"Why do we have to understand humans?" asked Betsy.

"If we understand them, dear, we can communicate with them better," said Hedy. "If we communicate with them better, we can enslave them more easily."

Whoa, thought Cheyenne.

"Why's Cheyenne helping us enslave humans?" asked Betsy. "Isn't that being disloyal to her own people?"

"Cheyenne is very sympathetic to our cause," said Hedy. "Also, she doesn't even know she's helping us. She's been hypnotized. When she returns to her home, she'll forget everything that happened here."

"How do you know she's really hypnotized?" asked Betsy.

"Let me prove it to you," said Hedy. "Cheyenne, in a moment I'm going to turn you into a rooster. When I touch you on the top of your head, you'll become a rooster." She walked over and touched Cheyenne on the top of her head. "I have just turned you into a rooster, dear. How do you feel?"

"Cock-a-doodle-doo," said Cheyenne in a flat voice. She flapped her arms.

The mutants giggled.

"That doesn't prove she's hypnotized," said Betsy. "How do you know she isn't faking?"

"What would convince you, dear?" said Hedy.

"Make her do something she'd never do if she wasn't hypnotized," said Betsy. "Something gross and disgusting."

"Gross and disgusting?" said Hedy. "All right." Hedy went to the desk, picked up an empty glass, and gave it to Betsy. "Spit into this glass," she said. Betsy spit. Hedy handed the glass to another mutant. "Spit into the glass," she said.

The mutant spit into the glass. Hedy had all the mutants spit into the glass. Then Hedy herself spit into it.

"Cheyenne," said Hedy, "you've had such a long walk through the woods to get here. You must be really thirsty, dear. Here's some delicious lemonade." She handed the glass to Cheyenne. "Drink it."

Oh, yuck! thought Cheyenne. *What do I do now?*

"She's not taking the glass," said Betsy.

"She will," said Hedy. "Don't worry."

What should I do? thought Cheyenne. *I can't drink their spit—that's too disgusting to even think about. But if I don't, they'll know I'm faking. Hedy will be furious. She might do something terrible to me. She might even kill me.*

Trying not to show any emotion at all, trying not to think about what she was doing, Cheyenne took the glass and drank what was in it.

The mutants howled with laughter. Cheyenne shuddered with revulsion. She almost

puked, but held back the retch with her teeth—ralphing would have been a terrible mistake. Waves of disgust spread over her, but she had done it, she had passed the test.

"How did that taste?" Betsy asked.

"Yummy," said Cheyenne in a flat voice. "I love lemonade."

The mutants howled with glee.

"Just because she drank spit doesn't prove she's hypnotized," said Betsy.

"No?" said Hedy. "What would convince you, dear?"

Betsy stared directly into Cheyenne's eyes. "Hedy," she said, "can humans who are hypnotized feel pain?"

"No," said Hedy. "They cannot."

"Then let's hurt her," said Betsy. "Let's see if she feels the pain."

Thanks a lot, Betsy, thought Cheyenne. *What am I going to do* now? *More important, what are* they *going to do?*

"How would you suggest we hurt her?" said Hedy.

"Break off one of her fingers."

No! thought Cheyenne.

"No," said Hedy. "I don't want any permanent damage."

"Then let me bite her."

"All right," said Hedy. "But don't pierce the skin. I don't want to see any blood."

"Why don't you?"

"I . . . do . . . not . . . wish . . . to . . . see . . . blood," said Hedy in a creepy voice. She turned to Cheyenne. "Cheyenne," she said, "Betsy is very fond of you. She wants to kiss your hand."

Cheyenne's heart raced in her chest.

"I don't like . . . being kissed by strangers," said Cheyenne in a flat voice.

"I can't see the harm in it," said Hedy. "It won't hurt you a bit. I have given Betsy permission to kiss you. Go ahead, Betsy."

Looking directly into Cheyenne's eyes, Betsy took her hand and bit it.

The pain was sudden, sharp, and swift. Cheyenne used every bit of strength and determination she could muster not to show any reaction. She might have blinked, but that was all. The pain continued.

"Okay, Betsy, that's enough," said Hedy.

Reluctantly, Betsy stopped biting. Cheyenne's hand throbbed with pain. She could see several tooth marks. From each one oozed a shiny bead of blood.

Hedy was annoyed. "Betsy, I see blood," she said. "Did I or did I not tell you I did not wish want to see blood?"

"I guess I goofed," said Betsy, smiling wickedly.

"You will pay for disobeying me, dear," said Hedy in her creepy voice. "Not now, but at a time when you least expect it."

"Oooh," said Betsy. "I'm scared."

"You may not be now," said Hedy. "But you will be when the time comes, I promise. Now then, are you satisfied that Cheyenne is in a trance?"

Betsy continued to stare at Cheyenne's face.

"I said are you satisfied now, Betsy?"

"I suppose so," said Betsy.

Yesss! thought Cheyenne.

CHAPTER 16

Never Go Home with Escorts Whose Faces Are Wrapped in Big Black Bandages

The escort was dressed in black and waited patiently until Hedy was ready. Its face, Cheyenne noticed, was hidden by a big black hat and wrapped in a wide black bandage. She hadn't noticed the bandage before. What was the purpose of the bandage? Was this ont's face disfigured even more than Hedy's had been in the fire at Mandible House? What did it look like with the bandage off? Cheyenne shuddered.

"All right," said Hedy, "you can take her home again. I don't think she'll wake up till she's back in bed. If she does, you know what to do."

The black-clad escort nodded and guided

Cheyenne out of the room and into the long tunnel that led to the mouth of the cave.

Cheyenne sneaked a look at the hand that Betsy had bitten. The blood from the tooth marks had scabbed over. The pain still throbbed. *I can't believe I didn't show anything when she bit me,* Cheyenne thought. *I can't believe I drank a glass of mutant spit. Ugh!*

When they reached the mouth of the cave, the two guards nodded to them as they passed. Once they were outside in the forest, the air was fresher and very fragrant.

Her escort turned right instead of left. Cheyenne was pretty sure that home lay to the left. But if she said anything, the escort would know something was fishy. She had too much invested in having everybody think she was still in a trance. She couldn't risk blowing everything by pointing out that they were going in the wrong direction.

Wally was relieved to see Cheyenne and her escort emerge from the cave. He'd been waiting and worrying for almost two hours. But then they turned right instead of left.

Left is the way back home, he thought. *Why are they turning to the right?*

He didn't know what was going on. Weren't they bringing her home as they'd done two times before? If not, where were they taking her? All he could do was follow them and stay out of sight.

Cheyenne's escort had her by the upper arm now, leading her gently but firmly through the forest. Cheyenne knew this wasn't the way back to the Spydelles' house. Where were they going? And at what point, if any, should she speak up?

The escort was pushing her through some bushes, pushing her toward . . . a car!

A tiny black French car, a Citroën 4CV, stood in a small clearing next to a narrow gravel road. The escort was opening the passenger-side door and motioning for Cheyenne to get inside. There was no reason she could think of not to, so she got in. The escort slammed the door, the sound muffled by the thick foliage that surrounded them. The escort went around to the driver's side, got in, and started up the engine. The car took off, going much too fast, branches whipping, scraping, and smacking at the vehicle as it sped down the road.

Within minutes the Citroën emerged from Dripping Fang Forest and turned onto the blacktopped interstate in the direction of Cincinnati. At that point the escort removed the big black hat, then unwound the thick black bandage. The face that emerged from beneath the bandage was covered with thick dark fur. The mouth was filled with rows of sharp white teeth.

The Master of a Thousand Disguises drove with one hand and lit up a stinky French cigarette with the other.

"Permit me to introduce myself," he said, inhaling smoke that stank like vomit. "I am known as The Jackal."

Hey, he's not even an ont, thought Cheyenne. *Why should I continue pretending I'm in a trance?*

"Nice meeting you," she said. "I'm Cheyenne Shluffmuffin."

"I know who you are," said The Jackal. "And you, of course, have heard of *me*."

"I'm sorry," she said. "I'm afraid I haven't."

"You're serious?"

Cheyenne nodded.

"My dear young lady," said The Jackal, puffing out his chest, "I am known on nine continents."

"There are only six," she said.

"Excuse me?"

"North America, South America, Africa, Australia, Antarctica, and Eurasia," she said. "Six."

"I beg to differ with you," said The Jackal. "Eurasia happens to be Europe *plus* Asia. *Two* continents there, not one. So that makes seven. Then there's . . . Greenland and, uh . . . Ireland."

"Greenland's not a continent, and neither is Ireland," said Cheyenne. "And I'm sorry, but Europe and Asia are never counted as more than one. So, six. But I think it's really nice you're known on six. By the way, who do you know in

Antarctica? I mean, does anybody actually live there besides seals and penguins?"

"Are you mocking me, young lady?"

"Not at all," said Cheyenne. "I was just wondering if there are any people in Antarctica."

"There *are* people in Antarctica," said The Jackal, enunciating every word. "There are at least *nine* of them. And they *know* me."

Wally, who'd seen Cheyenne drive off with the black-clad escort, returned to the Spydelles' house in agony. He felt like he'd eaten a dinner of black slime and needed to puke it up. *Somebody has kidnapped Cheyenne,* he thought, *and it's all my fault. He might have already killed her by now, or maybe he's only torturing her. Boy, do I hope he's only torturing her.*

He thought of waking up Edgar, Shirley, and Dad, then decided that there was nothing they could do about Cheyenne's disappearance till morning and why get them all upset? Wally slept fitfully, drifting in and out of disturbing dreams. Faceless figures dressed in black kept chasing him through the forest in small French cars. Cheyenne kept sinking in quicksand, arms flailing, screaming for his help.

Around seven o'clock he was awakened by the sound of a ringing telephone. Somebody else in the house must have answered it, because the phone quickly stopped ringing. Then Shirley appeared in the doorway of his bedroom.

"Wally, it's for you," she said, handing him the phone. She looked serious.

"Is it Cheyenne?" he asked excitedly.

She shook her head. "No."

"Then who is it?" he asked.

"He wouldn't tell me," she said. "Maybe he'll tell *you*."

"This is Wally," said Wally into the receiver.

"Listen carefully and do not interrupt," said the voice. "If you want to see your sister again alive, come to the Horace Hotchkiss Aquarium tonight at midnight. The back door will be unlocked. Come unarmed. Come alone. If you want to see your sister dead, then by all means bring the police or the FBI or anybody else you care to invite. Have you understood what I just said?"

"Who is this?" Wally demanded.

"Someone with whom you have unfinished business," said the voice.

"What's your name?" Wally shouted.

The person at the other end of the line hung up.

CHAPTER 17

All in Favor of Tearing Him to Pieces, Raise Your Claws

Six P.M. Wally, Shirley, Edgar, and Vampire Dad sat on hammocks in the living room. The sun had not yet set, but the thick forest that surrounded them admitted little light to the room. Shirley was crying softly. The guys were looking very grim.

"We're holding this meeting," said Wally, "because we all love Cheyenne and we want to be sure we're handling this kidnapping in the best way we can. I told you what the kidnapper said to me on the phone. Now tell me what *you* think."

"I don't understand why he didn't ask for

ransom money," said Dad. "What kind of a kidnapper doesn't ask for ransom money?"

"Maybe he just has a grudge against me personally," said Wally. "When I asked him who he was, he did say, *'Someone with whom you have unfinished business.'* "

"What kind of unfinished business could you have with anybody?" asked Shirley. "Is there somebody who doesn't like you?"

"Well, let's see now," said Wally. "There's the freaks at Dripping Fang Country Day, there's the giant slug who glows in the dark, there's all the man-eating wolves in the forest, there's half the orphans at Jolly Days, there's Hedy Mandible, there's the Ont Queen, and there's all of the onts . . ."

"I think we should call in the authorities—the police or the FBI or somebody like that," said Shirley.

"But the kidnapper warned us not to," said Wally.

"Those people are professionals, Wally," said

Shirley. "They handle this kind of thing all the time. We're amateurs. We've never handled this kind of thing before in our lives. We're only going to mess it up."

"I think we should all go over there and tear this guy to pieces," said Dad. "Look what we did to the Mandible sisters. I'd really like to sink my fangs into this guy—and not to drink his blood, in case that's what you're thinking. I have no ulterior motives. I wouldn't drink a single drop of it, I swear. I haven't tasted human blood in weeks."

"As much as I detest violence," said Shirley, "if we decide to take matters into our own hands, I would certainly be willing to inject this person with paralyzing venom."

"And I am more than willing to hurl toxic chemicals at him, as I did at Mandible House," said Edgar, "in case anyone remembers that—and in case anyone bloody well cares what I think."

"Of *course* we remember, Edgar, and of *course*

we bloody well care what you think," said Wally. "But we have to keep in mind what the kidnapper said about coming alone: *'If you want to see your sister dead, then by all means bring the police or the FBI or anybody else you care to invite.'*"

"But if we overpower him and tear him to pieces," said Dad, "then how can he kill Cheyenne?"

"He could have left Cheyenne with an accomplice," said Wally. "He could have said to his accomplice, 'If I don't come back, or if you don't hear from me by such-and-such a time, go ahead and kill her.'"

Everyone was silent, thinking his or her own miserable thoughts.

"I think we have no choice but for me to go to the aquarium alone tonight," said Wally.

Nobody answered.

CHAPTER 18

Never Meet a Kidnapper in an Aquarium at Midnight

It was nearly midnight. Vampire Dad brought the Spydelles' Land Rover to a stop outside the Hotchkiss Aquarium. The long, low building looked closed. It crouched there in the darkness,

lights glowing eerily in two windows like eyes of man-eating wolves.

"I still wish you'd let me come in there with you and rip this guy's throat out," said Dad.

"I know, Dad," said Wally, "and I appreciate the thought, but we just can't risk it. You know that."

"I suppose you're right," said Dad. "I wonder why he wants to meet you in an aquarium."

"Maybe he likes fish," said Wally, getting out of the car.

"Well," said Dad, "if you're not out of there in ten minutes, young man, I'm coming in after you."

"Better make it fifteen," said Wally.

Quietly shutting the car door behind him, Wally headed around to the back of the building. In an area where there were heavy metal Dumpsters and a row of sealed plastic trash cans, Wally spotted a steel door marked NO ADMITTANCE. With his pulse thundering in his ears, he turned the doorknob, opened the door, and stepped inside.

At first it was so dark he couldn't see a thing.

But the place smelled pretty bad, like rotting fish. Wally heard the steady thrum of heavy machinery. As his eyes gradually became accustomed to the dark, he saw that there were puddles of water on the concrete floor, and several coiled hoses.

He wondered how he was supposed to make contact with the kidnapper.

"Hello?" said Wally tentatively.

Behind him in the darkness, grinning wickedly, The Jackal waited, relishing the boy's discomfort.

"Hello?" said Wally again. "Anybody here?"

The Jackal poured several drops of chloroform onto a clean white handkerchief, then stepped forward and clamped it over Wally's nose and mouth. Wally struggled briefly, then slumped forward, unconscious.

The Jackal scooped him up in his arms and carried him across the room toward the tanks.

Sledge, the tank cleaner, had observed Wally's entrance and The Jackal's attack. *So this is his daredevil friend who fights crocodiles, grizzly bears, and great white sharks professionally—,* he thought, *a skinny ten-year-old boy.* Sledge didn't particularly like ten-year-old boys. On the other hand, he didn't particularly like being lied to, either.

The tank cleaner was definitely annoyed. *Am I annoyed enough to stop what is happening?* he wondered. *Or am I intrigued enough to wait awhile and watch what the creature might do with the boy?* It had been a long time since he'd watched the giant octopus dismember and ingest a living person. Perhaps too long.

CHAPTER 19

Okay, the Good News Is It's Not a Giant Snake

The shock of hitting the cold water snapped Wally right back into consciousness. As the water closed over his head, he blew air out of his nose and swam to the surface. His waterlogged jeans and sneakers made his legs feel like they weighed about eighty pounds apiece.

Although at first he couldn't quite recall what he was doing there, soon it all came back to him—entering the back door of the aquarium, then having somebody clap something nasty-smelling over his nose and mouth. So, if he was in a tank in an aquarium, he was probably swimming with some kind of fish. He wondered what kind he could be swimming with.

Angelfish? Clown fish? Zebra fish? He sure hoped it wasn't piranhas.

Something touched him ever so gently in the middle of his back. He felt it clearly through his T-shirt. He tried to turn and see what it was, but before he could, another something slithered around his chest. Something rubbery and very muscular, something that was tightening around him! An aquatic snake of some kind? An anaconda? And now another one was wrapping itself around his legs!

On his mental computer, Wally Googled anacondas and came up with: *the longest snake in the world, verified specimens thirty-three feet in length, with unverified reports of fifty and a hundred feet . . . a snake that doesn't bite but crushes its victim in its powerful coils, then unhinges its lower jaw and swallows its prey whole—even deer and jaguars.*

Struggling to keep his head above water, Wally tried to pry off the snake that was encircling his chest and found it was stuck to him with little round suction cups. *This is no snake,* he realized.

He looked up. The thing around his chest was pulling him through the water toward the head of the biggest octopus he'd ever seen in his entire life! The head was the size of a sumo wrestler! The eyes were the size of soup plates! Where all the fifteen-foot-long tentacles came together, Wally knew, was the creature's mouth and a hard, parrotlike beak that injected paralyzing venom! A definite bummer.

As soon as he'd dumped the unconscious boy in the water, The Jackal switched on his camcorder and began watching the drama in the tank through its viewfinder. *This is superb,* he thought, *my own private Animal Planet reality TV show. I had planned to give this tape to the Ont Queen to document Wally's death, but perhaps I* could *sell the footage to a TV production company. Unless, of course, the Assassins Code of Ethics forbids commercial exploitation of a hit?*

He continued to watch Wally's pathetic attempts to stay alive.

Silly me, thought The Jackal. *Why limit my*

experience of a death struggle by viewing it second-hand through an eyepiece? Holding the camcorder as steadily as he could, he alternated glimpses of action between the viewfinder and his naked eye. *Ah, so much more satisfying!*

When the two-legged dinner dropped into her tank, the giant octopus had been dozing in the rocky den at the bottom. Usually, the feeders served live lobster, oysters, crabs, clams, crayfish, shrimp, snails, squid, or scallops. So when she glided out of her den to learn what was on the night's menu, she was surprised to see something bigger than usual.

Eventually she recognized the surprise treat as the young of the species that fed her and cleaned her tank. Perhaps this young one was sick or defective, and they wished to get rid of it. Well, if it didn't taste too spoiled, she was willing to dispose of it for them.

CHAPTER 20

Take These Arms, I Want to Lose Them—Well, One of Them

The tentacle around Wally's chest was getting so tight he could scarcely breathe. Struggling to keep his mouth above water level, he jammed a hand into his jeans pocket and pulled out his Swiss Army knife. The tentacle was drawing him slowly but surely toward the creature's head. When it got him within range of the mouth and its flesh-dissolving saliva, he knew, that would be the end of him.

Wally was somehow able to pull a blade out of his knife. Without hesitation, he plunged it deep into the tentacle. Blue blood spurted. The tentacle didn't release its deadly grasp, but the angry octopus instantly turned bright red.

Wally plunged his blade into the tentacle again and again. More blue blood spurted, but he was still being drawn steadily toward the creature's head. He was just two yards away.

As the creature drew him underwater toward its open mouth, Wally managed to snatch a deep breath and yank the saw blade out of his knife. He began frantically sawing away at the tentacle. He glanced at the dial of his scuba watch. Ten minutes after twelve. The watch was no help to him, but the hours he'd practiced holding his breath underwater in the bathtub while his sister pounded on the door were maybe paying off.

When he was a foot from the animal's yawning mouth, the sawed tentacle at last completely separated from the octopus's head and its hold on Wally loosened. *So long, suckers,* he thought as it dropped away.

Wally's lungs were bursting. He had to get a gulp of air soon or he'd be forced to inhale water. Still holding his breath, he started swimming to the surface, but another tentacle smacked him so hard, he dropped his knife. It sank out of sight.

Dad waited in the Land Rover outside the aquarium. His eyes were fastened on the dial of the dashboard clock. It was now eleven minutes since Wally had gone inside. The boy had asked Dad to wait fifteen minutes before coming in after him. Should he respect his son's wishes or go in sooner? Like maybe now? Was Wally in trouble, or did he have things under control?

Dad decided to respect his son's request and wait a little longer. He turned on the radio. A tune from an earlier era flooded the car, "Full Moon and Empty Arms."

CHAPTER 21

You Really Do *Not* Want to Annoy a Vampire

As Wally's head broke the surface, he came face-to-face with the red head of the enraged giant octopus. Its hostile glare was more than Wally could bear. In desperation, he punched the beast in an eye.

A cloud of black ink bloomed suddenly in the water like a small thermonuclear explosion. The octopus had released enough ink to camouflage herself and confound her attacker.

Splashing madly, Wally turned and began swimming frantically in the opposite direction.

"Infernal idiot!" said The Jackal. "Now look what you've done!"

Stupid brat! thought Sledge. *Ink released in a confined space the size of this tank will be toxic to everyone—especially the animal! I* cannot *have this octopus die!*

Sledge rushed toward the octopus tank. He grabbed a black rubber hose off the floor and turned it on. Cold water under pressure shot out of the nozzle, causing the hose to convulse like an injured snake. With a firm grip on the writhing hose, he hauled it up the ladder to the top of the tank and shot the jet of cold water into the cloud of toxic ink, trying to dilute it.

A few yards away, Wally reached the edge of the tank and grabbed on to it with both hands. He pulled himself up and tried to climb out.

The Jackal quickly put down his camcorder, hurried to the bottom of the ladder, and prepared to intercept the wet boy.

As Wally began swinging his left leg out of the water, he felt something slimy slither around the leg that was still in the tank. The tentacle began to tighten around his ankle, but he violently kicked the tentacle free, then hurled himself over the edge of the tank, nearly missing the top step of the ladder.

That was when Dad came in through the back door.

"Dad!" yelled Wally.

"Wally!" Dad shouted. "Thank god you're safe!"

"That's the jerk who kidnapped Cheyenne!" Wally pointed down at The Jackal.

Dad turned to the grinning assassin. "Is she still alive?" Dad demanded.

"Oh, your daughter is quite safe, Mr. Shluffmuffin," said The Jackal. "Which is, unfortunately, more than I can say for *you*!"

The Jackal reached inside his trench coat and withdrew a Navy SEAL combat knife with a black steel blade.

Dad glided swiftly up to The Jackal and bared his fangs. With one hand, he gripped The Jackal's knife hand so tightly the assassin screamed like a frightened girl and dropped his weapon. With his other hand, Dad gripped The Jackal's throat.

"Listen to me quite carefully," said Dad. "Unless you tell me where my daughter is immediately, I shall sink my fangs in your jugular and suck you so dry of blood, you'll crumble like a saltine cracker."

"T-t-take it easy," gasped The Jackal. "Sh-she's in a locker at the Greyhound bus station."

"You put her inside a *locker*?" said Dad, tightening his grip.

"A b-b-big *comfortable* locker," said The Jackal, barely able to form words. "And I'll t-t-take you there, I p-p-promise —just please don't b-b-bite me."

Unseen by Dad, Sledge had quietly picked up a scuba speargun and was aiming it at Dad's back.

"Dad! Duck!" yelled Wally, but it was too late.

Fsssshhhh . . . thutttttttt! The spear shot out of Sledge's speargun and landed in Dad's back, impaling him like a chunk of lamb on a shish kebab skewer.

CHAPTER 22

You Can't Say We Didn't Warn You About Annoying a Vampire

Dad seemed surprised. He stared at the three-foot length of spear sticking out of his chest. Then he whirled on the tank cleaner, the front end of the spear smacking The Jackal in the head and knocking him to the ground. Dad pulled out the spear and snapped it in half.

Sledge raised both hands and began backing away from Dad.

"Easy now, big fella," he said, "I don't want any trouble with you."

"You don't?" said Dad. "You have an interesting way of showing that."

Dad stuck two fingers up the tank cleaner's nose and lifted him a foot off the ground. "Wally!" Dad called out. "Has this person caused you any discomfort tonight?"

"Not really," said Wally.

"Is there anything he can get you while he's up?" Dad asked.

"Well, I lost my Swiss Army knife in the tank," said Wally.

"If it's not too much trouble," said Dad pleasantly to Sledge, "could you possibly find a moment to retrieve my son's knife?"

"Yes . . . anything . . . yes . . . ," Sledge whimpered.

"I would so appreciate that," said Dad, lowering the tank cleaner to the floor.

While Dad was occupied with Sledge, The Jackal began creeping quietly toward the door. Wally bounded to the bottom of the ladder and floored the assassin with a flying tackle around the legs.

"Ooooff!" said The Jackal, falling hard.

Massaging his sore nose, Sledge grabbed his snorkel and lurched up the ladder. Then he took a deep breath and dropped into the tank.

The giant octopus had recovered her composure at losing a tentacle and was comforting herself with the awareness that it had probably already begun growing back. Frustrated at having her dinner treat escape, she was also hungrier than usual. Her gaze fell on the tank cleaner, who had reached the inky water at the bottom of the tank. *Hmmm.*

CHAPTER 23

Our Larger Lockers Are Really Quite Comfy

The Land Rover pulled up in front of the Greyhound station. Then Dad, Wally, and The Jackal got out of the car.

"You'll see, Mr. Shluffmuffin," said the Jackal. "Cheyenne is not at all uncomfortable in that locker."

"Get into that bus station this minute and get me my daughter," said Dad, "or I'll drain you of fluids."

The Jackal scurried into the bus station.

Except for an elderly lady snoring loudly on one of the wooden benches, the inside of the Greyhound terminal was deserted. The large room was brightly lit and smelled strongly of urine. On the far side of the room was a bank of battered blue-metal lockers.

The Jackal walked toward the lockers, with Dad and Wally following closely behind him. "Here we are, here we are," said The Jackal.

He took out a little card and glanced at the note he'd made to himself. Then he grabbed the combination lock and spun the dial. A moment later the locker door swung open.

Cheyenne sat scrunched up inside the tiny space.

"Cheyenne!" cried Wally.

"Cheyenne!" cried Dad. "Are you all right?"

Cheyenne opened her eyes and smiled.

"Hi, Wally. Hi, Daddy. Hi, Mr. Jackal," she said.

Wally helped her out of the locker. She seemed very stiff and had difficulty standing upright at first.

"Are you okay?" Wally asked.

"To tell you the truth," she said, "it wasn't too interesting in there. But I do think it was a valuable experience. I had a lot of time to think."

Dad and Wally hugged her.

1-800-VAMPIRE

"See, Mr. Shluffmuffin?" said The Jackal. "I told you that locker wasn't so uncomfortable after all."

"Then show me," said Dad.

"What?" said The Jackal.

"Get inside and show me."

"Normally I'd like nothing better," said The Jackal, "but I happen to have an important engagement later tonight, so I'm afraid it's out of the question."

Dad grabbed The Jackal by the shoulders and tore open his trench coat to expose his neck. Dad bared his fangs and snarled impressively. "Get in that locker immediately."

The Jackal squeezed into the locker, and Wally jammed its door shut behind him.

"Mr. Shluffmuffin, sir?" called a small voice in the locker.

"Yes?" said Dad.

"When do you think I might be getting out of here, sir?" called the voice.

"Just as soon as the Cincinnati police can find a larger place to put you," said Dad.

CHAPTER 24

All Right Then, How Would *You* Define Employed?

"So, Mr. Shluffmuffin," said the social worker, sinking down in the hammock and consulting her clipboard, "it has now been exactly two weeks. Have you placed your children in school as I instructed you?"

"Yes, ma'am," said Dad. "They now attend the Dripping Fang Country Day, right here in the forest."

"Excellent," she said, noting this on her clipboard. "And how did the job hunting turn out?"

"In a word," said Dad, *"exciting."*

"You went out on many interviews."

"Oh yes, ma'am," said Dad. "Many, many

interviews. Lots and lots of very gratifying interviews with many, many wonderful employers."

"Excellent," said the social worker. "And you've found a job."

"Three employers are so crazy about me," said Dad, "I honestly don't know how I'm going to be able to choose one without totally breaking the hearts of the others."

"So you *haven't* gotten a job," said the social worker.

"If by 'haven't gotten a job' you mean 'haven't yet signed on the dotted line' or 'haven't yet filled out the forms for the health insurance' or 'haven't yet signed up for the office Secret Santa pool,'" said Dad, "then, no, technically, I guess I haven't yet gotten a job—although I tell you I'm so close, so very close, I can almost taste it."

The social worker looked hard at Dad and chewed her lower lip. "Nobody wanted you because of the fangs and the wings, huh?" she said.

"Right," said Dad, the air leaking out of him like a deflated balloon.

The social worker stood up.

"I'm sorry, Mr. Shluffmuffin," she said. "You seem like a pretty nice guy for a vampire. But I'm afraid I must now order that your children be returned to the orphanage."

CHAPTER 25

Vampire Dad Can't Go On Like This

A somber group had gathered in the Spydelles' living room to say farewell.

On one side stood Dad, Shirley, Edgar, Cheyenne, and Wally. On the other side stood the social worker and Hortense Jolly. Hortense was the only one whose eyes were dry. Cheyenne sniffled and blew her nose. She and Wally clutched little plastic bags that held toothbrushes, underpants, Wally's rescued Swiss Army knife, Grandma Gloria's salt-and-pepper shaker, and the peanut-butter-and-jellied-veal sandwiches that Shirley had thoughtfully prepared for the trip back to the orphanage.

For several moments the leaky faucet dripping—*plip-plip-plip*—in the kitchen sink was the only sound.

"I say, Miss," said Edgar to the social worker, "isn't there any way my wife and I might adopt these dear children?"

The social worker sighed and shook her head.

"Professor Spydelle, the Child Welfare Bureau has a definite policy against giant spiders as adoptive parents," she said. "They've been very clear about that."

"This is barbaric, I tell you," said Edgar, shaking his head. "Utterly barbaric!"

Hortense grabbed each child tightly by the wrist. "Come along, children," she said with forced jollity. "If we hurry we can just make it back to Jolly Days in time for dinner."

Cheyenne and Wally flung themselves into the arms of Dad, Shirley, and Edgar, sobbing openly, tears spilling down their cheeks as they kissed good-bye. Then Hortense dragged the twins outside.

Shirley, Dad, and Edgar went to the door and watched them climb into the Jolly Days school bus. Hortense started up the engine and the bus lurched out of the driveway. The social worker got into her sad, rusty old Chevy and drove off as well.

Dad was the first to break the silence.

"I can't go on like this, I tell you—I can't!" he cried.

"You can't go on like *what*?" said Edgar, drying his eyes with a folded pocket silk.

"Like *this,*" said Dad. "Look at me. I'm a member of the walking dead. A vampire with fangs, wings, and a barely controllable thirst for human blood. I can't get a job. I can't get custody of my own children. I want to be alive again! I want to be a father to my son and daughter again! Give me another shot of your Elixir of Life, Edgar! It's my only hope!"

"Is it?" said Edgar. "And where is *my* hope?"

"Excuse me?"

"Where is *my* hope of being a father?" asked Edgar. "Your children, who once claimed to love me and Shirley more than you and *begged* us to adopt them, now *admit* they love you more. Do you not think that stings?"

"Well, I suppose it stings, Edgar," said Dad, "but surely—"

"And," Edgar continued, "having lost the love of *your* children, my only recourse now is to mate with Shirley and have children of our own, and accept the fact that she, like all spider wives, will kill me after mating—something that you, being lucky enough to be married to a dead human instead of to an enormous spider, would know nothing about. Do you really expect me to feel sorry for *you*?"

"Uh, well, no, Edgar. Under the circumstances, I guess not," said Dad. "So is that a *no* on the Elixir of Life?"

CHAPTER 26

You *Can* Go Home Again, But They're Still Serving Gruel with Boogers

Hortense Jolly pushed Cheyenne and Wally into the orphanage dining room and bonged her heavy brass bell with a soup ladle.

"Attention, orphans of Jolly Days!" said Hortense. "Our dear friends the Shluffmuffin twins have returned. They have failed once again to find anyone who wants them."

"Hey, Sniffles and Stinkfoot, how did you screw it up *this* time?" shouted Rocco the bully.

Wally walked over to Rocco and punched

him in the stomach. Then all of the orphans sat down to a dinner of stale bread crusts and a thin gray soup that looked like mucus with little green floaty things in it that looked like boogers.

CHAPTER 27

Why, Grandma, What a Big Babushka You Have

The two Cincinnati policemen entered the Greyhound bus terminal and headed for the lockers.

"What is it we're supposed to be finding in this here locker?" asked Officer Nietzsche. He was short and feisty-looking and had a bristly moustache.

"Some kind of kidnapper, they said," answered Officer Schopenhauer. He was very tall and had terrible posture and a face like a sad basset hound.

"What's a kidnapper doing in a bus station locker, Art?" said Officer Nietzsche.

"I don't know, Fred," said Officer Schopenhauer. "I'm just going by what they told me on the radio, okay?"

The two cops found the right locker.

"This is the one, Fred," said Schopenhauer. "What was that combination again?"

"Let me see here," said Nietzsche. "It says forty-three, thirteen, sixty-seven."

"Right," said Schopenhauer. "Okay, forty-three . . . thirteen . . . and sixty-seven."

The lock popped open. The policemen opened the locker. Scrunched into it was . . . a little old lady in a babushka and a tattered dress.

"What th—?" said Schopenhauer.

"Who are *you,* ma'am?" asked Nietzsche.

"Please, sor," said the old lady, climbing painfully out of the locker and trying to straighten up. "No spicka da Hinglish."

"This here don't look like no kidnapper to *me,*" said Nietzsche.

"Me neither," said Schopenhauer.

"You might as well go, ma'am," said Nietzsche.

"Please?" said the old lady, cupping her hand to her ear, as if their speaking too softly was the problem.

"He said . . . you're . . . *free* . . . to . . . *leave,"* said Schopenhauer, bending down and speaking slowly and loudly.

"Oh, sankyou, sor," said the old lady. She gathered up her skirts and hobbled out of the bus station.

"I think that was the right thing to do, don't you?" said Nietzsche, staring after her.

"Absolutely," said Schopenhauer. "I must say, Fred, those foreign women are getting furrier-looking every day."

The instant the old lady got outside the bus station, she tore off her babushka and her tattered dress, revealing the black leather trench coat of the Master of a Thousand Disguises, known on at least six continents as well as Greenland and, possibly, Ireland.

He would, of course, be back.

NO
PARKING

What's Next for the Shluffmuffin Twins?

Now that The Jackal has been thwarted a second time, he's plenty frustrated and furious. Will he concoct a new plan to kill poor Wally that's even grosser and more sadistic than feeding him to a four-hundred-pound octopus? And what could possibly be grosser and more sadistic than feeding him to a four-hundred-pound octopus?

Having again tasted the pleasures of family life, Cheyenne and Wally can't bear returning to the cruel life at the orphanage. Will the twins discover that it was Hortense's jealousy and greed that ripped them out of the arms of their beloved father and the many arms of the Spydelles? And what if somebody new shows up at Jolly Days and wants to adopt the twins? Somebody as bad as the Mandible sisters—or even worse?

How will Dad, and Edgar and Shirley Spydelle, cope with their grief at losing Cheyenne and Wally? Maybe Vampire Dad will make another attempt at suicide, this time with a bullet that's more than silver plate, or with a stake through his heart that's solid wood instead of wood-grained Formica. Will Edgar, embittered that the twins prefer their real father, do something really stupid? Will Shirley, in her despair at being childless, make good on her threat of having a litter of spiderlings—and then be forced to eat Edgar in the process?

Cheyenne will probably be summoned back to the Ont Queen's cave to tutor the mutant children. If so, what new gross and disgusting tests will Betsy think up to see if Cheyenne is faking being in a trance? And what can Cheyenne and Wally do to halt the Ont Queen's plan to enslave humans and end life on Earth as we know it?

You can*not* possibly afford to miss the next thrilling volume of Secrets of Dripping Fang, Book Seven: *Please Don't Eat the Children*!

DAN GREENBURG writes the popular Zack Files series for kids and has also written many best-selling books for grown-ups. His seventy books have been translated into twenty languages. To research his writing, Dan has worked with N.Y. firefighters and homicide cops, searched for the Loch Ness monster, flown upside down in an open-cockpit plane, taken part in voodoo ceremonies in Haiti, and disciplined tigers on a Texas ranch. He has not, however, personally encountered any zombies or giant octopuses—at least not yet. Dan lives north of New York with wife Judith, son Zack, and many cats.

SCOTT M. FISCHER glided through high school doing extra-credit art assignments for math teachers, which is kinda boring stuff to draw. Next he went to art school, where he learned to paint even more boring things—like flower vases. However, he swears that since then he has drawn nothing but cool stuff—like oozy, drooling monsters, treacherous villains, and the occasional flower vase . . . that has fangs and eats flowers for breakfast!